Enid Blyton's
NODDY
and the Bumpy Dog

Illustrated by Edgar Hodges

Purnell

One sunny morning Noddy got up bright and early. "Come on, car," said Noddy, "we'll go and see if we can find someone who wants to be taken to the railway station this sunny morning."

"Parp-parp!" hooted the car happily, as they drove out into the road. Noddy waved to his next-door-neighbour Mrs Tubby Bear as he rode by.

She called to Mr Tubby Bear, who was planting seeds in the garden. "There goes Noddy again, what a busy fellow he is," she said.

Noddy had a busy morning. First he took Mr Noah to the station to meet Mrs Noah, who had been to stay with her aunt. Then he took Miss Toy Rabbit to the market to buy some pink ribbon to match her dress.

"Come and help me choose, Noddy," said Miss Toy Rabbit. Noddy was just thinking that he didn't know much about choosing ribbons, when he noticed his friend Tessie Bear walk by. She was also shopping.

"Look," he said. "There's Tessie Bear, she will help us! Tessie, Tessie, can you help us to choose some ribbon to match Miss Toy Rabbit's dress?"

So Tessie Bear went with Miss Toy Rabbit and Noddy to look for the ribbon. The market place was very busy and it took them a long time to

choose the right colour ribbon, but eventually they did. Miss Toy Rabbit was so pleased that she offered to buy Noddy and Tessie Bear an ice-cream from the little shop at the end of the market place. After such a busy morning Noddy felt quite hot and bothered, so he was pleased to rest for a while in the colourful ice-cream shop.

They were just finishing their ice-creams, when they heard a loud crashing noise on the road outside.

"Wuff-wuff-wuff! Wuff-wuff-wuff!"

"You shouldn't have got in my way! It was your fault!"

"Oooh-wuff-oooh-wuff-oooh-wuff!"

Noddy ran to the door of the shop. Whatever could have happened?

A toy dog sat barking in the middle of the road outside the ice-cream shop, while a sailor doll picked his bicycle up off the pavement.

"Fancy running across the road just as I was coming down the hill at top speed!" he shouted angrily. "Wuff-wuff," barked the dog sadly, holding up his front paw to everyone as if it hurt.

"Serves you right," said the sailor doll. "Perhaps you'll stay off the road in future!" Then he jumped on to his bicycle and rode away at top speed.

The dog limped over to Noddy, and held out his paw. Tessie Bear stroked and patted the little toy dog's head.

"I'll bandage your paw for you," said Noddy, taking out his nice clean handkerchief. "Hold it up. There, you keep this bandage on for a day or two and I promise you your paw will soon heal."

"Wuff-wuff-wuff," said the dog, putting his head on one side, and pricking up his ears.

"I wonder if he belongs to anyone," said Tessie Bear. "If he does, they'll look after him. Go on, find your master!"

"We've got to go home now!"

"Take care of that paw!" shouted Miss Toy Rabbit as the car drove off.

"I don't expect we shall ever see that dog again," said Noddy sadly, as he drove to Miss Toy Rabbit's house.

But he was quite wrong.

Two days later, just as Noddy was cleaning his car, someone came running in at the front gate and knocked him over.

"Oooh – what's that? Oh, it's you, dog!" said Noddy, getting up. "Is your paw better?"

"Wuffy-wuff!" barked the dog, and he put his paw on Noddy's knee to show him that it was quite better.

"Wait a minute, I've got a piece of bread and butter left over from breakfast, would you like it?" asked Noddy.

"Wuffy-wuff-wuff!" answered the dog, and it jumped around Noddy excitedly.

"It's very difficult to walk with you galloping round me like this," said Noddy, pushing the dog away. "Now where did I put that bread and butter?"

Noddy looked in his bread bin and found a big crust and held it out. The dog snapped it up, and swallowed it in one gulp. "What a gobble!" chuckled Noddy. "You couldn't even have tasted it!"

The dog ran all around the little house, sniffing every where. He even jumped into Noddy's chair and sat there. "Wuff-wuff!" he said, and looked so pleased that Noddy couldn't help liking him. Noddy went out to finish cleaning his car. He was getting ready for work.

"Now I'm going out to look for some passengers, so you must go home, dog," said Noddy. "I suppose you have got a home to go to?"

The dog barked sadly and walked away down the lane.

Noddy had a very good day, and picked up lots of passengers. The little car purred along happily, it was very pleased when Noddy had a busy morning. Noddy felt so pleased when he arrived home, that he called over the wall to Mrs Tubby Bear.

"I've earned a lot of money in fares today Mrs Tubby Bear, listen to the shiny coins jingling in my pocket!"

"My word!" said Mrs Tubby Bear. "You sound rich, Noddy. Now don't go round jingling that money for everyone to hear.

There are goblins about, you know. If they hear that you've so much money in your little house they might come to steal it!"

"Don't worry Mrs Tubby Bear" laughed Noddy. "I'll put it away carefully. Now I'm going to have my tea."

Noddy put his car away, and then went into his little House-for-One to have his tea. He was very very hungry. While his kettle boiled, he buttered some bread and spread it thickly with potted meat.

He was just about to take his first bite of the potted meat sandwich when he heard a noise outside. Someone was scratching at his door. Then he heard a voice, a very doggy voice.

"Wuff-wuff-wuffy-wuff. WUFF! WUFF! WUFF!"

"If it isn't that dog again!" said Noddy. "Well, it will be nice to have a bit of company at tea-time. Come in, dog!"

He opened the door and the dog bounced in, leaping up at Noddy in delight. Noddy fell down at once, and the dog jumped on top of him and licked him all over.

"Please don't!" said Noddy. "I like having a bath at night, not at teatime. Stop licking me you naughty dog!"

The dog smelt the potted meat sandwiches on the table, and ran off to sniff at them. He turned and looked at Noddy with great big eyes.

"Wuff," he said, mournfully. "Wuff-wuff."

"Oh, so you're hungry again, are you?" said Noddy, getting up.

The dog leapt at him and down went poor Noddy again on to the floor. "Don't do that!" said Noddy, crossly. "You really are a naughty dog, you're always bumping into me. If you haven't got a name, I shall call you Bumpy, because you bump in to people all the time. Oh no, please don't lick me again! Look – have a sandwich!"

The dog took the sandwich from Noddy and swallowed it in one gulp. Then he ran over to Noddy and knocked him over again.

"BUMPY! Will you stop bumping into me and knocking me over?" said Noddy angrily. "You'd better go home. I'm getting a bit tired of this." Noddy opened the front door and sent him out.

By now it was Noddy's bedtime so he put on his pyjamas and got in to bed. He blew out his candle and went to sleep thinking about his busy day and of all the bright new shiny coins he had earned.

But Noddy was so tired that he had forgotten to lock his door when he turned Bumpy out. In the middle of the night someone came creeping up the garden path. When they tried the door and found it open, they crept in and took Noddy's bag of shiny coins.

The next morning when

Noddy discovered that all his money had been stolen he rushed next door to Mrs Tubby Bear's house.

"We'll have to tell Mr Plod," said Mr Tubby Bear. Soon Mr Plod was in Noddy's little house.

"It's one of those goblins from the Dark Wood, I'm afraid Noddy. It's not much use my going there to hunt for your money because the thief will have buried it somewhere by now."

"I worked so hard for it too!" sighed Noddy sadly. "Oh no! Here's Bumpy again. Look out, Mr Plod!"

Bumpy came running in at the open door. He saw Mr Plod and leapt up at him joyfully. Any friend of Noddy's was a friend of his! Mr Plod almost fell over, but just saved

himself in time. His helmet shot off and rolled under Noddy's bed.

Bumpy ran after it at once, bumping in to Noddy and sending him tumbling on to the floor. He dodged outside into Mr Tubby Bear's garden where he saw Mr Tubby's row of seed-labels marking his neat row of seeds. Aha! Someone had been digging there! Bumpy was sure that Mr Tubby Bear had buried a bone or two under those labels! And, before anyone could stop him, he was scratching up all the rows of seeds, and scattering the labels everywhere!

"My word!" said Mr Plod. "He's dug up all your seeds. That dog's a menace. I'd better take him and lock him up."

"No! No, please don't," shouted Noddy. "Bumpy didn't mean to be naughty. I expect he thought Mr Tubby had buried some bones in his garden – not seeds. Look, Bumpy you MUST go away. Mr Plod has to find out who stole my money, and you keep getting in the way."

"Wuffy-wuff," said Bumpy, sadly, and he backed into Mr Tubby Bear who nearly fell over!

"I'm not helping you to get your money back," said Mr Plod, in a huff. "Not until you get rid of that dog, anyway."

"But how can I get rid of him?" asked Noddy.

"He'll follow you anywhere. Why don't you take him for a walk in the woods," said Mr Plod. "While you're away we can get on with the search for your money."

"I'll do it right away," said Noddy. "He's a good dog really. It's a pity that he's such a bumpy dog!"

Mr Plod marched off down the road, looking cross, and Mr Tubby Bear began to rake over his seed-bed, looking even angrier.

"Come on, Bumpy," said Noddy sadly. "We'll go to the market and buy you a big bone."

"Wuff-wuff!" said Bumpy, and wagged his tail happily.

Noddy drove to the market, with Bumpy sitting proudly beside him in the car. Whenever Noddy hooted the horn, Bumpy barked loudly.

"Look – there's Tessie Bear. I'll hoot and give her a wave," said Noddy.

"Parp-parp!" said the car. "Wuffy-WUFF!" barked Bumpy, and Tessie Bear looked round in surprise. She ran to the car and patted Bumpy.

"Oh – you've got that dear little dog with you. Is his paw better?" she asked.

"Yes, but he's a nuisance, I can't seem to make him go away Tessie," said Noddy. "He's dug up all Mr Tubby Bear's seeds, and Mr Plod said I should take him for a long walk in the woods so that he could get on with the search for the stolen money."

"What stolen money?" asked Tessie Bear.

"Oh Tessie, I forgot to tell you. Last night someone entered my House-for-One and stole the bag of shiny coins I'd saved."

"Oh dear, I am sorry!" said Tessie Bear.

"Mr Plod couldn't start the search for the robber because Bumpy kept getting in everyone's way. He suggested that I take Bumpy for a long walk in the Dark Wood," said Noddy.

"Can I come too?" said Tessie Bear.

"Oh yes, that would be lovely," said Noddy. "Bumpy, sit in the back, please. No, DON'T lick Tessie Bear's bonnet off."

On their way through town Miss Tessie Bear asked Noddy to stop off at the market for a moment. "Won't be a minute," whispered Tessie Bear. She came back a few minutes later with a bone neatly wrapped up, some sandwiches and cakes, and two bottles of fizzy red pop.

"As it's such a nice day, I thought that we could take a

picnic along too," said Tessie.

"What a good idea!" chuckled Noddy.

"Woofy-woof!" barked Bumpy Dog.

"Parp-parp!" agreed the car.

They drove deep into the Dark Wood and when they got to a sunny clearing, they stopped the car and got out.

Before Noddy could unwrap the bone Bumpy jumped up excitedly, and knocked Noddy over with a bump.

"Goodness me – if you were my dog, I'd have to sit down all the time to stop you bumping me over," he laughed. "Here's your bone. Now go and have fun while we have our picnic!"

Bumpy took the big bone and trotted off with it. He found a good place under an old tree. He put down the bone and began to dig, sending the earth

flying all over Noddy and Miss Tessie Bear.

Just then, to everyone's surprise, a goblin jumped out from behind the old tree.

"Hey! Stop that," he yelled. "Don't dig under my tree – you bad dog! Stop it at once!"

The goblin ran up and tried to stop Bumpy. Bumpy growled at the goblin, then he jumped up at him and knocked him over.

Bumpy carried on digging – and then Miss Tessie Bear shouted and pointed at the hole Bumpy had been digging.

"Something's buried there! Oh Noddy, I'm sure it's something that goblin has hidden there!" she shouted.

Noddy ran over to look, and the goblin tried to push him away. Bumpy jumped up at the goblin at once and knocked him over again. "Wuff-wuff-wuff!" barked Bumpy, sounding very angry. He wasn't going to let anyone push his friend Noddy about!

Noddy saw something buried deep down in the hole that Bumpy had dug.

"It's my bag of money!" he shouted. "This goblin must have stolen it last night and buried it here."

"Oh you bad goblin!" said Miss Tessie Bear. "Look out Noddy – he's running away. Catch him!"

But it was Bumpy who caught him. He could run much faster than the goblin and he soon caught up with him and bumped him over.

Noddy gave Bumpy a big hug. "I am glad Tessie bought you a bone to bury, we'd never have found my money if she hadn't! And to think you chose the very spot where it was hidden. Isn't he clever Tessie?"

"He's the cleverest dog in the world," said Miss Tessie Bear, "and I like him very, very much."

"We'll go back to Toy Village, and we'll drop this goblin off at the police station," said Noddy. "Mr Plod will be pleased to see him."

Away they drove through the Dark Wood, back to Toy Village. Bumpy ran behind the car all the way to make sure that the naughty goblin didn't try to jump out and run away again.

Everyone in Toy Village was most astonished to see Noddy, Tessie Bear and a goblin driving slowly down the street in the little red and yellow car, with Bumpy following behind, his tail wagging hard.

"Look!" cried Miss Fluffy Cat. "Whatever is going on?" Everyone followed the car and Bumpy to the police-

station, and Big-Ears, who was riding by on his bicycle, followed too. Whatever was Noddy up to now?

"Hey, Mr Plod! Mr Plod! I've brought you the goblin who stole my money last night!" shouted Noddy.

Mr Plod came out of the police-station at once.

"Ha! I've been looking for this rascal for a long time! Why it's the same goblin that stole Miss Fluffy Cat's silver tea-spoons last month!"

"And look, Mr Plod – here's my bag of money! Bumpy found it for me. Isn't he a good dog?" said Noddy happily.

"Yes," said Mr Plod. "But he's a dog I'd get tired of very quickly. Take him away. If he jumps up at me once more I'll lock him up with the goblin."

"You'd better come with us, Bumpy," said Big-Ears.

"WUFF-WUFF!" barked Bumpy excitedly.

"Let's go to the cake-shop Big-Ears, and I'll tell you all that's happened," said Noddy. "You can come too, Bumpy. I'll buy you a treat for finding my money for me."

Very soon they were all sitting in the cake-shop and Bumpy was very proud to have a chair to himself. His tail wagged so fast that it knocked a cake out of Tessie Bear's hand.

"Bumpy – PLEASE keep still," chuckled Noddy, then he told Big-Ears all that had happened. Big-Ears was astonished.

"Has Bumpy got a home of his own?" he asked.

"No, he hasn't," said Noddy. "I'd like him to live with me – but he's so very, very bumpy. I mean – I'd be sitting on the floor most of the time if I had him. Anyway, Mr Tubby Bear wouldn't like him living next door, because Bumpy dug up all his seeds. Couldn't you look after him Big-Ears?"

"I'm afraid not," said Big-Ears. "Whatever do you suppose my old cat Whiskers would say? It's a puzzle, isn't it? Bumpy has been so good and helpful that he really ought to have a good home!"

"I know!" said Tessie Bear suddenly. "I'll look after him. My uncle can make him a kennel at the bottom of our garden. I'll teach him to be good, too."

"Well – I don't think that will be very easy!" laughed Big-Ears. "But he'll certainly make a good pet. Would you like to live with Tessie Bear, Bumpy?"

"Wuff!" barked Bumpy happily. "Wuffy-wuff-wuff!"

"That's settled then," said Noddy.

"I promise to take him for long walks and bring him to see you every day," said Tessie Bear. "Come on then, Bumpy – let's go and build you a nice kennel!" Tessie waved goodbye and walked off with Bumpy, her new dog, walking beside her.

"Bye, for now Bumpy, look after Tessie won't you?" shouted Noddy.

"Wuffy-wuff! Wuffy-wuff!" answered Bumpy as he trotted off merrily down the street.